HAIR-POCALYPSE

written by GEOFF HERBACH

illustrated by STEPHEN GILPIN

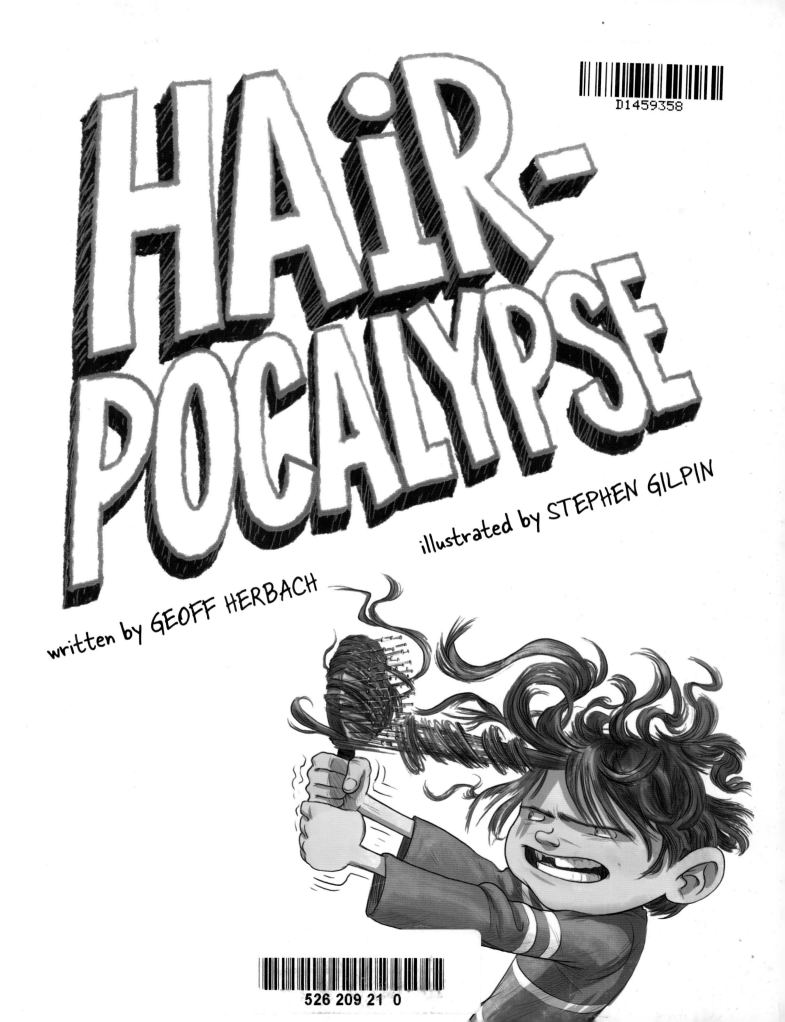

First published in 2017 by Curious Fox, an imprint of
Capstone Global Library Limited, 264 Banbury Road,
Oxford, OX2 7DY – Registered company number:
6695582

www.curious-fox.com

Text copyright © 2017 by Geoff Herbach
Illustrations copyright © 2017 by Curious Fox

The author's moral rights are hereby asserted.

Illustrations by Stephen Gilpin

ISBN 978 1 78202 747 8
21 20 19 18 17
10 9 8 7 6 5 4 3 2 1

A CIP catalogue for this book is available from the
British Library.

Printed and bound in China.

For my mum, who had a grubby kid. — G.H.

For my sister, Sarah. My main mane wrangler. — Stephen

Aidan Allen was a grubby kid. His clothes were always **wrinkled**, his shoes were always **untied** and he always seemed to have grass stains on his knees.
But none of that was the problem.

The real problem was that Aidan Allen's hair was COMPLETELY out of control. It wasn't just messy. It seemed to have a mind of its own.

"LIE DOWN, HAIR! WHY CAN'T YOU BEHAVE?"

His hair seemed to MOVE.
His hair seemed to SHRUG.

That is NOT possible,
Aidan thought.

Aidan reached into a drawer and pulled out
his mum's big blue brush. But when he brushed,
the bristles immediately became tangled in
his greasy locks. His hair seemed to be
GRABBING the brush.

At the breakfast table, Dad looked up from
his phone and shook his head in dismay.

"Aidan, your hair is crazy. You have to do SOMETHING."

"I already tried," Aidan said.

"Better try again," Dad said.

Aiden caught sight of the clock.

"There's just no time," Aidan said as his hair grabbed his spoon and dumped his cereal on the floor!

On the bus, Aiden's hair tied itself into **three bows**. Aiden knew everyone was staring at him. He tried to pretend nothing was happening.

But at school, Kate Benton spotted Aidan and his crazy hair right away. It had formed **airplane wings** on the sides of Aidan's head. There was NO WAY Kate would stay silent.

"Look at Aidan Allen's hair!" she shouted.

But from the first bell on, his crazy hair did ANYTHING but stop.

During art class, Aidan's hair grabbed some paintbrushes and splattered paint everywhere!

At lunch, Aidan's hair formed a giant, dangerous raptor
that blew over Noah Foster's milk — right onto his trousers.

"STUPID, STUPID HAIR!"

At break, Aidan's hair turned into an **octopus-like** creature. It wrapped around Kate Benton and her friends and pulled them into a nearby mud puddle.

"YOU'RE THE WORST HAIR IN THE WORLD!"

After break, Aidan felt defeated, and his hair was WORSE THAN EVER. Telling his hair what to do wasn't working. Yelling at his hair wasn't working either. He took a **big breath** and talked to his hair.

Immediately his hair formed into a magnificent mass of curls.

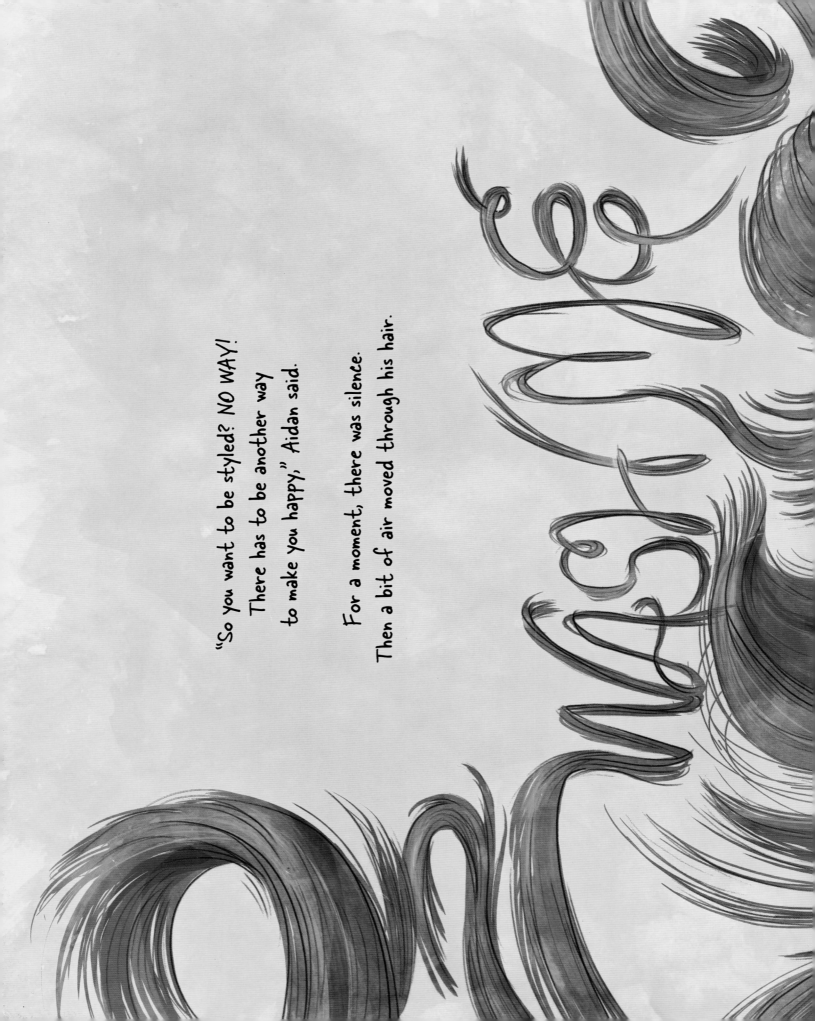

"So you want to be styled? NO WAY!
There has to be another way
to make you happy," Aidan said.

For a moment, there was silence.
Then a bit of air moved through his hair.

On the bus home, Aidan and his hair discussed a plan to fix their issues. Aidan was exhausted. Clearly his hair was **exhausted**, too. It lay lifeless and flat, looking even worse than usual.

That night, Aidan took a shower before his dad asked him to. He sang a song and sudsed up.

Aidan and his hair had come to an **agreement**. Aidan would wash every weekday, but weekends were his days to be TOTALLY GRUBBY.

At the breakfast table the next morning, Dad looked up from his phone and shook his head in amazement.

"Your hair looks FANTASTIC!"

"Thanks!" Aidan replied.

"But your shirt is dirty and your shoelaces are untied," his dad said.

"I'm a grubby kid, Dad. I'm doing the best I can right now."

"OK, then," Dad said.

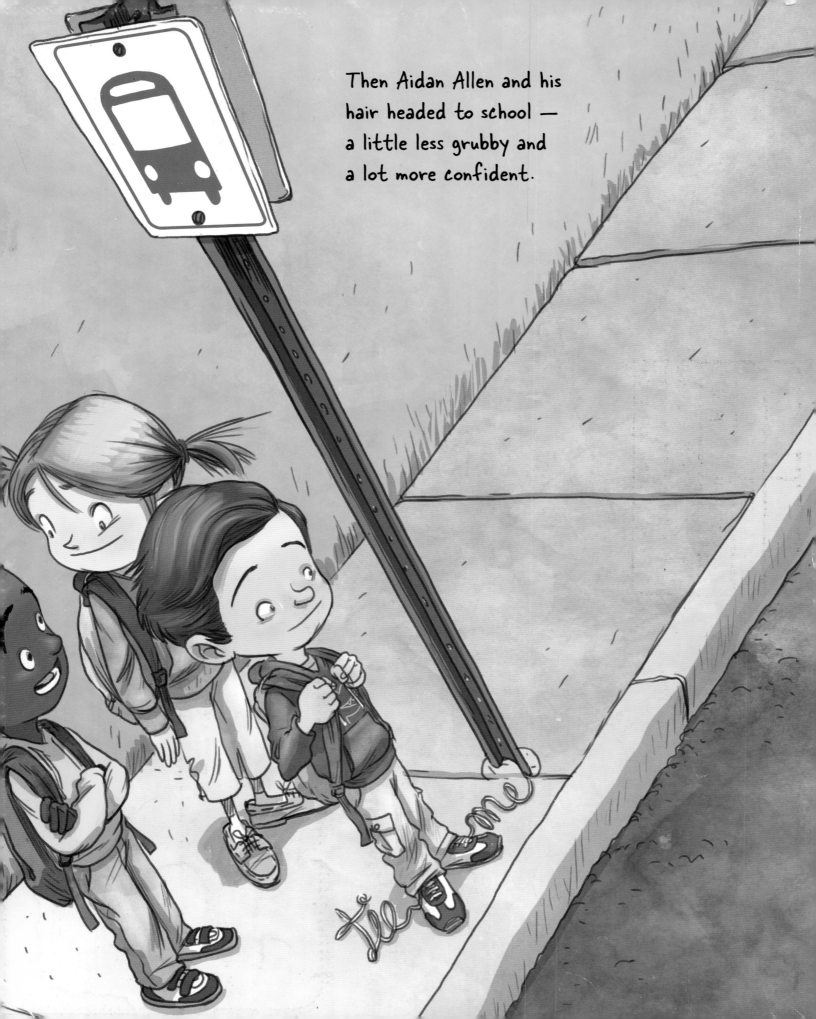

Then Aidan Allen and his
hair headed to school —
a little less grubby and
a lot more confident.